SPOOKY STORIES

Three Stories in One

PENELOPE
LIVELY

MARY
HOFFMAN

GILLIAN
CROSS

EGMONT

We bring stories to life

Dracula's Daughter was first published in Great Britain 1988
Debbie and the Little Devil was first published in Great Britain 1987
The Monster From Underground was first published in Great Britain 1990
Published in one volume as *Spooky Stories* 2008 by Egmont UK Limited
239 Kensington High Street, London W8 6SA

ISBN 978 1 4052 4230 1

1 3 5 7 9 10 8 6 4 2

A CIP catalogue record for this title is available from the British Library

Printed and bound in Singapore

CONTENTS

Mary Hoffman

Dracula's Daughter

Illustrated by Chris Riddell

For Ertaç and the
other Lea Valley juniors who
encouraged me to finish it
M.H.

For Katy
C.R.

Chapter One

ANGELA WAS A model child in every way. Of
course her arrival was unusual. Mr and Mrs
Batty were not expecting a baby – they were
expecting a parcel of plants they had ordered
for the garden. So they weren't surprised when
there was a ring at the doorbell and a basket
dumped on the step. Only in the basket was a
baby girl with brown eyes and black hair. Mr
and Mrs Batty forgot all about the plants and
looked after the baby instead.

She looked such a little angel, they decided
to call her Angela. On the first anniversary of

her arrival through the post, the baby was adopted and became Angela Batty. There were no problems in her babyhood. She walked and talked on time, ate up her greens, tidied up after her games and did not pull the cat's tail.

The trouble really began on her fifth birthday. In the bundle with Angela there had been an envelope saying:

"This child was born on 31st October. Open this letter on her 5th birthday."

Of course, Mr and Mrs Batty had wanted to open the envelope straight away, in case it contained a clue about her parents, but they somehow felt it would be unlucky to look inside before the given date. So after Angela's birthday party, when all her friends had gone home clutching their loot bags, her parents solemnly took down the envelope and opened it.

That was all. Mr and Mrs Batty were a bit disappointed and they rather objected to this grand lady referring to Angela as 'her' daughter.

'She's ours now – all legal,' said Mrs Batty firmly.

'Besides,' said her husband, 'if she was a rich lady, as it seems, why did she have to go dumping her child on a doorstep?'

For a while everything went on as normal. Angela went to school, made friends and was called a good girl by her teachers. Several of her friends began to get wobbly teeth and talk about the tooth fairy and ten pences. So Angela's parents were not surprised when she got her first gap. But, when the new tooth grew to fill the gap, they *were* a bit worried. All the other children had nice square teeth, but

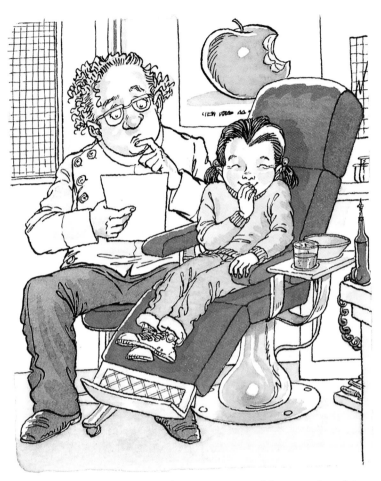

Angela's came to a sharp point, like a shark's.
The dentist was puzzled, but not really worried
– he reckoned Angela's tooth could be filed
straight when she was older. But even he
declared himself beaten by the time Angela
was in top infants and had a mouthful of sharp
pointed teeth.

Some of Angela's old friends were no longer allowed to come and play at her house, their parents didn't like the look of those fangs.

Other odd things had started to happen too. Angela had always been good about eating her vegetables, but now she became almost entirely a meat-eater. She loved beefburgers, chops, roast Sunday joints and steaks if she could get them. She would tuck happily into the sort of meat that other children didn't enjoy, like liver and kidney. She also enjoyed beetroot, blackcurrant juice, red cabbage and raspberries.

When Mr and Mrs Batty saw their beloved daughter lifting her smiling face from a bowlful of raspberries, with her pointed teeth stained all red, they exchanged nervous looks.

Other strange things happened too. Mrs Batty took a course in French cookery and began to be adventurous about sauces. But the day she came home with her first bunch of garlic,

Angela let out a scream and hid in the garden shed. She wouldn't come back indoors until Mrs Batty had thrown the garlic out. The Battys hadn't got Angela christened as a baby and now they were beginning to wonder if that would help. They invited the vicar round one afternoon. All went well until Angela came in from school. She took one look at his dog-collar and cross and ran for the shed again.

The mystery was settled once and for all that evening. After Angela had gone to bed, Mr and Mrs Batty got out the envelope and read the card inside it again. Mr Batty had been doing the crossword in the newspaper and now he pointed to the signature with a shaking finger.

'My dear – it's an anagram. Mix up the letters in CLARA DU COTUN and what do you get? COUNT DRACULA!'

Chapter Two

IT DIDN'T TAKE the Battys long to get used to having a vampire in the family. After all, Angela didn't show any signs of wanting to bite anyone. But one thing her parents had definitely decided was that if her original father ever *did* turn up, they would not let him take her away from them.

'If she *is* a vampire,' said Mrs Batty, which was a thing she never talked about except to Mr Batty, 'at least if she stays with us she will be a nice well brought up vampire, who brushes her teeth after every meal.'

But the teeth weren't the only problem. It was an unusually warm autumn and the Battys left the bedroom windows open all night to cool the house down. One night Mr Batty could not sleep for the heat and he went to look in on Angela. He was back in his own bedroom in a flash, shaking his wife awake.

'Wake up, my dear!' he shouted, 'she's gone! Angela's not there!'

But when Mrs Batty had woken up and run down the corridor, she found Angela sleeping peacefully in her bed, with her usual angelic smile.

'You must have been dreaming,' she told her husband crossly, 'waking me up and frightening me for nothing like that!' But she closed Angela's window all the same.

October came in as warm as September and the Battys began to prepare for Angela's seventh birthday party. She had asked for a proper Hallowe'en party, with dressing up, a cauldron cake and pumpkin lanterns at the windows. Her parents were nervous – it seemed to them to be asking for trouble. On the other hand, lots of normal children were going to Hallowe'en parties too.

'It's bound to appeal to her nature,' said Mr Batty. 'Angela being what we think she is. But she's a good girl. I don't think she can be *all* vampire, you know.'

Angela certainly looked all vampire on the night. She wore a short black cloak that Mrs Batty had made for her, and had circled her eyes with red lipstick. She had rubbed green eye shadow – bought specially – all over her face. When she smiled her fangy little smile, her parents couldn't help shuddering.

'I do hope we're doing the right thing with this party,' said Mrs Batty, as Angela rushed to open the door. She let in another vampire, two witches, an imp and a wizard.

'You look terrific, Angela!' said one of the
witches, who was her friend Emma from
school, 'Really scary!'

After they had been joined by some more vampires and a spook or two, the party really got going. As the games were played and prizes won, most of the children acquired long red fingernails or white plastic fangs. Angela began to look just like everyone else. The house had a pumpkin lantern at every window and even Mrs Batty wore a tall black hat. So they were visited by a specially large number of trick-or-treat gangs that night. Mrs Batty was prepared, with a big bowl of currant-cakes she had made, right by the front door.

So when the doorbell rang yet again, she already had a cake in her hand as she opened the door to a tall black-haired man in an opera cloak, who looked just like Count Dracula.

Chapter Three

'GOOD EVENING!' SAID the man who looked like Count Dracula. 'Can I come in?'

Mrs Batty stood frozen in the hall, the cake in her hand. Just then her husband popped his head out of the living room.

'Oh good,' he said, 'I see the entertainer's here. Dressed for the part too! Come in then Mr . . . er?'

'Count,' said the man.

'Mr Count,' said Mr Batty, 'the children are all ready for you.'

"Mr Count" gave a ghastly smile and walked into the Batty's living room. Mrs Batty watched silently in horror, unable to move or speak. The cat streaked through the hall and out through the front door. Mrs Batty automatically closed it and went into the living room. The children were wild about the entertainer.

'Coo, Angela,' said her friend Darren, 'he isn't half realistic. Looks just like the real thing! Watch out for your neck!'

The entertainer didn't tell jokes or do tricks.

But every time he spoke or looked at the children they cheered and laughed. All except Angela. She was watching him with a queer look in her eye. And Mrs Batty was watching her.

"Mr Count" was watching everyone. He hadn't thought it would be so hard to recognise his own daughter, but all these little humans looked like vampires to him.

When he said, 'Who wants to come with me to my castle?' all the children put up their hands and shouted 'Me! Me!' Except one. And that one really *did* look like a vampire – the teeth were very natural, even though all that green stuff was obviously false.

The doorbell rang again. Mrs Batty saw the tall dark stranger moving towards her beloved daughter and felt something snap inside her. 'Angela!' she shrieked as she rushed between them.

The man turned on her with flashing eyes and fangs bared. He looked as if he was going to sink them into her plump pink neck. The children went very quiet and then there was a rustling sound. Angela had spread out her arms under her black cloak and flapped steadily up to the ceiling.

The "entertainer" took his eyes off Mrs Batty to watch his daughter proudly as she swooped round the room. Mr Batty was nowhere to be seen. Mrs Batty picked up a plastic sword that the "wizard" had brought and held it upside down in the shape of a cross, right in front of the man in the black cloak.

'If only I had some garlic,' she muttered.

'Come down, Fangella!' called the tall dark man. 'I've come to take you home. I see you are a credit to me.'

'Over my dead body!' cried Mrs Batty angrily, waving the plastic sword.

The man flinched, but said menacingly, 'That could be arranged.'

'Oh no you don't,' said Angela firmly, hanging upside down from the lampshade.

'I don't want to go to your horrid damp old castle with its spiders and rats. I want to stay here, where there's central heating and a nice cuddly cat.'

'But Fangella, you are my daughter!'

'Don't you dare call her that,' yelled Mrs Batty. 'Her name is *Angela* and she is my daughter now! She's adopted.' She took the adoption certificate, which she always carried in her pocket and waved it in the tall man's face, never letting go of the sword.

'She's not a Dopted, she's a Vampire!' shouted the man. 'I left her here nearly seven years ago, when I – er – had to go away for a while. And now I've come back to collect her.'

'I'm not going,' said Angela. 'You tried to bite my mother!'

The man gave a nasty laugh.

'I *did* bite your mother, Fangella, long ago. She was another one just like this, but she turned out to be too tough for me.'

Angela gasped. 'You mean I'm only *half a vampire?*'

'Yes, but your mother got away when I stole you and found some other human to help her. Between them they had me followed and locked up in a crypt with a strong spell on the door. I couldn't escape till your mother died. She never found out where I left you and now I claim you as my own. It's a vampire's father that really matters – by the way where *is* that silly human that thought I was a party magician?'

Angela looked round wildly for Mr Batty but he wasn't there. The other children were all looking up at Angela on the ceiling with their mouths open.

'I'm not going,' said Angela again. 'I'm only half a vampire and I'm going to choose to be the other half.'

'We'll see about that,' said the tall man. 'Just you wait till I get my fangs on you.' Then he spread his cloak and aimed himself at the lampshade.

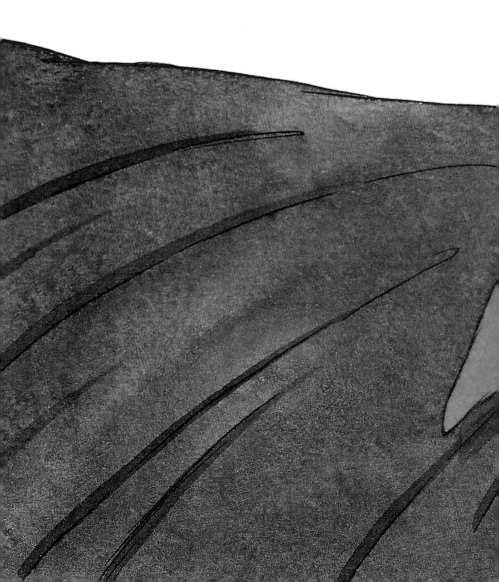

Chapter Four

AS HE LAUNCHED himself up towards Angela,
the man in black suddenly gave a loud scream
and fell to the ground at the sight of Mr Batty,
in the doorway, holding a large tree with
orange berries on its branches and earth
dropping from its roots. Behind him stood
another tall man in evening dress.

'Gotcha, you daft old bat!' said Mr Batty
triumphantly, and prodded the cloaked figure
with the tree. The shrieks and moans became
louder. 'We don't want you or any of your kind
ever coming to bother our Angela again! This is
a rowan tree and I know you vampires can't
bear them. I'm going down to the garden
centre tomorrow to buy up their whole stock
and I'm going to plant them all round the house!

Now be off with you!' Mr Batty motioned to the window and Mrs Batty opened it.

The man who looked just like Count Dracula dragged himself up onto the window-ledge and sat hunched there with his black cloak drooping down like a tattered old umbrella.

'So this is all the thanks I get,' he hissed up at Angela. 'A fine vampire you've turned out to be!'

'Half vampire,' corrected Angela, still upside down.

'Very well,' he said, 'stay here and eat your rice-pudding and go to Sunday school and knit the cat a pair of bootees if that's what you  want. You'll never get another chance like this. You would have had a much more exciting life with me!' Then he launched himself out of the window and flapped away into the night. Angela landed neatly on the floor right way up and gave a bow.

'Come on, dear,' whispered Mr Batty, putting down his tree and starting to clap. Mrs Batty got the message and clapped loudly. Soon all the children were clapping and cheering wildly.

'That was really *wicked*, Angela,' said Darren admiringly. 'How did you do the flying bit? And who *was* that geezer?'

'Oh just a distant relation on a flying visit,' giggled Angela.

'I'll never forget tonight,' said Mrs Batty, when the guests had all gone home and she and her husband were drinking their cocoa.

'When did you realise he wasn't the entertainer?'

'When I let the real one in, of course,' said Mr Batty. 'He caught on really quickly and helped me dig up the rowan.'

'That *was* a bit of luck,' said Mrs Batty. 'I didn't know we had a rowan tree in the garden.'

'We didn't,' said Mr Batty grimly, 'I pinched it from next door's garden. I expect they'll think it was the trick-or-treaters.'

'Well it would be hard to explain why you'd done it,' said his wife. 'But I'm really proud of you – and of Angela.'

'And I'm proud of you love, facing that old Count with nothing but a plastic sword.'

'You know one thing though, dear,' said Mrs Batty, 'he made me think it might be a bit dull for Angela living with us. We *are* a bit set in our ways.'

'Still, she chose us didn't she?' said her husband, licking the cocoa froth from his lips. 'She can't think we're too boring. But I'll try to be more adventurous if you like. What do you want me to do?'

'How about a nice holiday?' said Mrs Batty. 'We could go somewhere a bit different at Christmas.'

Mr Batty smiled. 'All right, dear. You get some brochures and we'll take our Angela off to somewhere exotic. Only mind – nowhere near Transylvania!'

Debbie
and the
Little Devil

PENELOPE LIVELY
Illustrated by Valeria Petrone

To Gaby and Massimo

V.P.

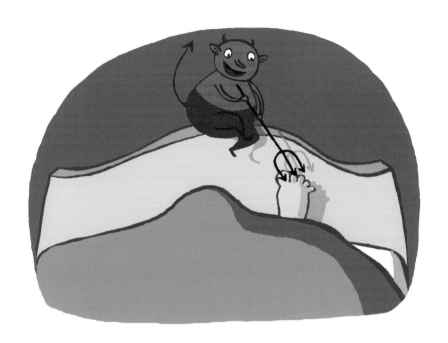

Chapter One

THE FIRST TIME Debbie saw the devil he was sitting on the end of her bed with one knee crossed over the other, humming to himself and prodding Debbie's foot with a long black fork. The devil was about eighteen inches high and as red as a hot coal. He had a long tail, two neat horns on his head and little black eyes. It was two o'clock in the morning.

Debbie sat up and said 'Stop poking my foot, do you mind!'

'Maybe,' said the devil. 'We'll see. I've got a job for you. You be a good girl and do what I say and we shall get on fine.'

'Are you a ghost?' asked Debbie.

'Certainly not! Nasty common things, ghosts. Upstarts. Ghost indeed!'

'Then what are you?'

'I'm a devil,' said the devil. He swished his tail and grinned. 'The real thing. Consider yourself lucky. Not many people get a look at me these days. Five thousand years old, I am!'

'I'm eight and a half,' said Debbie.

'Well, that's something to be going on with, I suppose,' said the devil. 'Now, let's get down to business. You know the cat next door? I want you to tie a tin can to its tail and then throw stones at it.'

'Certainly not!' said Debbie. 'That would be cruel and wicked and stupid and . . . and pointless.'

The devil scowled. He opened his mouth and blew a plume of bright red flame. 'I think it would be funny.'

'Well, I don't,' said Debbie, 'And don't smoke in my bedroom.'

The devil swished his tail again, which gave out a shower of little sparks, just like a firework. 'All right, then. Here's another idea. That old lady who lives opposite – you know, the one who walks with a stick. I want you to put a banana skin on her front doorstep so she'll step on it when she comes out and fall over.'

'You're *pathetic*,' said Debbie. 'You're so stupid you're pathetic. I'm almost sorry for you.'

The devil glared at her with his little black eyes and his tail fizzed away making blue and green and gold sparks.

'Spoilsport!' he snarled. 'You're hopeless, you are. No fun at all. Children aren't what they used to be.'

'I don't think I like you,' said Debbie.

'I'm not here to be liked,' snapped the devil. 'Just you wait and see.'

 At that moment Debbie's mother opened her bedroom door. The devil hissed and spat and blew another plume of flame and then he shrivelled up and vanished.

Debbie's mother came into the room and said she'd heard something – was there anything wrong? Debbie explained that there had been a small red devil sitting on the end of her bed, poking her foot and blowing fire at her. Her mother tucked her up again firmly and said, 'What a funny dream, dear. Now turn over and go to sleep again – it's the middle of the night.'

Then she went downstairs to check that she hadn't left the cooker on, because there was such a peculiar hot smell around the house, and when she had seen that all was well she went to bed again.

The next night the devil was back. Debbie woke up with a jump and there he was, grinning and humming and prodding with his fork. 'Go away!' she cried furiously.

'Shan't!' said the devil. 'We've hardly begun. Now listen to this. I want you to go downstairs and play around with some lighted matches so the house catches fire. Wouldn't that be fun!'

'You're horrible and nasty and *stupid*!' said Debbie. 'GO AWAY!'

'Sticks and stones may break my bones, but unkind words can't hurt me!' chanted the devil.

Debbie sat up. She reached for the glass of water by her bed and threw it at the devil as hard as she could. Debbie was rather a good shot so the glass hit the devil fair and square in the middle. It went straight through him and landed on the floor, where it broke. There was water everywhere.

The devil laughed and laughed. 'See!' Then he got smaller and smaller until he vanished and in the morning Debbie had to explain to her mother about the broken glass and the spilled water. She explained exactly and truthfully. Her mother was cross. She was cross about the broken glass but even more, she said, about making up silly stories.

Chapter Two

THE NEXT TIME the devil appeared was when Debbie was on her way home from school. There he was sitting on a wall at the end of her street. Nobody was paying any attention at all to him. A woman walked past him and the devil reached out with his fork and poked her in the side with it, and the woman slapped herself as though maybe she'd been stung by a wasp and walked straight on.

When Debbie reached him the devil said 'Wotcha!'

'I'm not talking to you,' said Debbie.

'But I'm talking to you,' said the devil. 'You won't get away with it like that. I'm older and wiser and cleverer than you are and I always win.'

'Bet you don't!' said Debbie, annoyed.

'Bet I do!' retorted the devil. 'Try me and see. What are you good at?'

Debbie thought. 'Jumping.' This was true. She'd won first prize in long jumping at the school sports and she was pretty good at high jumping too.

'Right!' said the devil. 'You see that pile of plastic rubbish bags there? Let's see who can clear that and land furthest on the other side. You first.'

Debbie stepped back and took a good run at the rubbish bags. She went flying over them but she'd gone at it a bit too fast and when she landed she tripped and came down on her knee. There was a nasty graze and quite a bit of blood. Trying not to cry, Debbie got up to watch the devil.

The devil rushed at the rubbish bags. When he was a yard away he jabbed his fork into the pavement and used it to give himself a huge push off. He came flying over and landed on his feet a yard further than Debbie. 'Easy!' he said. 'Ten out of ten to me. One out of ten for trying, to you.'

'You cheated!' howled Debbie. 'You used that thing of yours! You pole-vaulted! That wasn't fair!'

'Fair?' said the devil, 'Who's talking about fair? We're talking about winning. I told you I always win. Now you've got to do what I tell you or else. Go into the corner shop and nick some sweets.'

'I will not,' said Debbie. And she ran straight home where her mother plastered her knee but scolded her for fooling around in the street.

After that the devil really dug himself in at Debbie's home. Sometimes he woke her up in the night and at other times he'd suddenly appear, sitting up on the kitchen cabinet making faces at her or perched on the stairs or hanging from a tree in the garden. 'Whoo-hoo!' he'd say. 'Remember me?' Debbie's parents neither saw nor heard him. They walked straight through him. And Debbie was told off for talking to herself and being silly.

Chapter Three

THERE WAS WORSE than that, though. Things happened, when the devil was around. People dropped things and fell over and blamed each other and lost their tempers. One morning he stuck out his fork when Debbie's mother was bustling around the kitchen; Debbie's mother tripped up and dropped the tray she was carrying and scolded Debbie for getting in her way and everyone was cross with everyone else for the next half hour.

'That was your fault,' said Debbie to the devil, who was warming his toes on top of the cooker. 'You're beastly.'

'Sticks and stones . . . ' began the devil.

'Oh, BE QUIET!' shouted Debbie. 'I know all about that. But you won't always get it your own way, you'll see.'

'I always have,' said the devil, swishing his tail so that sparks flew all over the place. 'What's so special about you? I always win, remember. Who jumped furthest?'

'All right,' said Debbie. 'We'll try something else. And if I win you go away forever. Right?'

The devil swished and grinned.

'That's the bargain,' he said. 'I'm safe enough. What's a bit of a girl like you against someone five thousand years old who knows everything in the world.'

'Everything?' said Debbie.

'Absolutely everything,' said the devil.

'All right,' said Debbie. 'What does the Queen have for breakfast?'

'Fried snails,' said the devil promptly.

'She does not!'

'Prove it!'

'You're ridiculous,' said Debbie 'Very well then – what's black and white and read all over?'

The devil scowled and swished and sparked. His eyes flashed. 'Um . . . ' he said. 'A . . . The . . . Um . . .'

'A newspaper!' said Debbie triumphantly.

The devil hissed like a steam engine. He blew out a great tongue of flame.

'And what's the difference between an elephant and a post-box?' cried Debbie.

The devil glared. He opened and closed his mouth. 'An elephant . . .' he began, 'A post-box is . . .'

'Try posting a letter in an elephant and you'll find out!' shouted Debbie. 'And now tell me what's the highest mountain in the world? And who's the president of the United States of America? And how far away is the moon?'

But the devil had had enough (which was just as well since Debbie didn't know the answer to the last question herself). He huffed and puffed until he looked like a fat toad sitting there on the cooker. He sparked and flamed and then vanished with a pop, leaving behind the most dreadful smell of rotten eggs and burnt cabbage and drains. Debbie's mother telephoned for both the plumber and the electrician, neither of whom could find anything wrong, so there was more bad temper all round.

Chapter Four

AND THE VERY next day the devil turned up in the car, on the way to visit Aunt June. Debbie's father was driving and her mother was in the passenger seat and Debbie was in the back, and all of a sudden there was the devil too, sitting beside her with his fork propped up against his knees.

'You can't come to Aunt June's,' said Debbie.

'Try and stop me,' said the devil.

'What, darling?' said Debbie's parents, both at once.

'Nothing,' said Debbie, wearily.

The devil quite spoiled the outing. There he was, trailing around behind Debbie all day, making rude remarks, sitting on the sideboard all through dinner, poking the fruit in the fruit bowl with his fork – and none of the grown-ups knew a thing about him. He behaved very badly. He interrupted and jumped around the room and at one point he even started singing, in a high cackling voice that of course only Debbie could hear. Eventually she couldn't stand it any more.

'SHUT UP!' she cried.

'Debbie!' said her mother. And everyone stared at her and all she could do was mutter, 'I didn't mean you . . . ' which was no help at all. The devil perched on the windowsill and laughed.

'I'm not afraid of you, you know,' said Debbie to the devil on the way home. 'I'm just *bored* by you.' The devil was lolling on the back seat of the car, with his feet on the window ledge. His tail hung down against Debbie's leg. She gave it a push; it was like putting your hand right through a piece of red velvet.

'I don't exactly think you're a bundle of fun, either,' said the devil. 'As children go, you're a dead loss.'

'Then why hang around like this?'

The devil yawned. 'Because one's got a job to do.' And he went to sleep, snoring loudly.

Chapter Five

THE DEVIL WAS a bad loser, Debbie discovered. He challenged her to game of Scrabble and when Debbie started winning the devil turned all the letters into black beetles. They ran about the board and ruined the game.

'Don't *do* that,' said Debbie, 'That's my Scrabble game Aunt June gave me for Christmas. Now look at it!' The beetles ran round and round the table and the devil sulked.

'Oh, you're just *babyish* . . . ' said Debbie. 'All right, I'll let you win, but get rid of those beetles.' The beetles vanished and the letters came back and the devil scored three hundred and fifty-six and sat there grinning.

She beat him at cards, too. Snap and Rummy. So the devil turned the cards into dead leaves and Debbie's mother came into the room and wanted to know what all that rubbish was doing all over the floor. The devil, by then, had whisked up onto the curtain rail and was swinging by his tail, spitting fire.

'Have you been touching the matches, Debbie?' said her mother, sniffing.

When she had gone Debbie said to the devil, 'All right, then. You can win but next time I choose what we play, or I'm not playing at all.'

'You've got to play,' said the devil, 'That's what it's all about.'

'What do you mean?'

'It's what I do,' said the devil, 'I 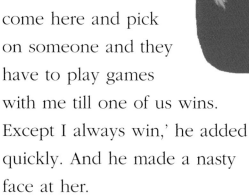 come here and pick on someone and they have to play games with me till one of us wins. Except I always win,' he added quickly. And he made a nasty face at her.

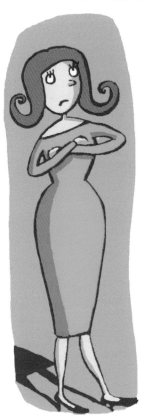

'Suppose you don't?' said Debbie. 'I already proved you don't know everything in the world. I beat you at Scrabble. And cards too, except you cheat.'

71

The devil fizzed his tail around. 'I don't know what cheat means. One does what one does. I'm just better at doing things than you are.'

'We'll see about that,' said Debbie. 'Two can play at that game.'

'All right,' said the devil. 'Let's get serious, then. No more messing about. Best of three. And then you have to do what I say for ever and ever.'

'If you win,' said Debbie. '*If* . . . '

She looked hard at him and the devil squinted back with his squinny black eyes and sent out little forks of fire from his red mouth.

'And if *I* win . . . ' said Debbie, 'then what?'

The devil spat and hissed. 'All right,' he said, 'all right. I'll stick to the rules. Such as they are. You win and I'll go.'

'Cross your heart?' said Debbie.

The devil laughed.

'All right, then – swear on that fork thing of yours.'

'Swear,' said the devil, 'And I can't get more honest than that. It was my dad's, that was, and his dad's before that.' He patted his fork fondly with one red paw. 'There! Sworn! But I'm wasting my time. I'll win. You'll see.'

'We'll see,' said Debbie.

They were in the kitchen. The devil hopped down from the back of the chair on which he had been sitting and rubbed his hands with enthusiasm.

'So . . . What shall we start with? How about a race? Simple flat race. From the back door to the end of the lawn and back.'

Debbie looked at him. She was more than twice as tall as he was; her legs were much longer. Wasn't it obvious that she would win? What was the devil up to?

'No funny business?' she said sternly.

'No funny business,' said the devil. His tail swished; sparks showered the floor.

I don't trust you, Debbie thought. I don't trust you one little bit.

They went out into the garden. 'Back doorstep is the start and finish post,' said the devil. 'Right?'

'Right,' said Debbie.

They lined up. 'One, two, three . . . go!' cried the devil.

Debbie sprinted. She was way ahead at once.

Just before she got to the end of the lawn she
looked back. There was the devil, pounding
away a couple of yards behind, his eyes flashing
and his tail whisking, looking like a huge spider.

Debbie turned at the rose bed and began to
sprint back. Halfway she felt a rush of air.
The devil flew past her, like a hot wind . . .
Whoosh!

And fly was exactly what he did. There on
his back had sprouted a pair of little black
wings. When Debbie got to the back doorstep

he was crouched down wriggling around. The
wings shrank and shrank and vanished into the
back of his neck.

'CHEAT! CHEAT! CHEAT!' shouted Debbie.
'You said no funny business.'

'Funny business?' replied the devil. 'What's
funny? I'm not laughing. Bad luck,' he added.

'Well tried and all that.' He rubbed his hands.
'One down, two to go. Now what? How about
some more jumping?'

'No,' said Debbie. 'It's my turn to choose.
We'll do throwing.' She knew she was a good
shot. 'We'll put a stick in the middle of the lawn
and see who can throw a quoit over it from
here. Best of three.' And before the devil could
say another word she had arranged the stick
and was handing him the quoit. 'You start.'

The devil scowled. You could see him
thinking away like mad. 'Go on,' said Debbie.
'You're not *scared*, are you? I thought you
always won?'

The devil flung the quoit. It flopped down a yard from the stick. Debbie threw; she was so jumpy she missed too. The devil grinned and took the quoit again. He threw . . . and the quoit went spinning past the stick. The devil jumped up and down and thrashed his tail on the grass.

Debbie aimed carefully. The quoit landed neatly over the stick. The devil, hissing now, ran to pick it up. He squinted at the stick . . . aimed . . . and threw. The quoit knocked the stick over and landed on the far side of it. The devil howled with rage.

'Last round!' said Debbie. She took a deep breath and threw, and plop! . . . again the quoit landed fair and square over the stick. She looked at the devil and the devil looked at her.

'Your go,' said Debbie.

The devil blew himself out like a ball. His spidery arm holding the quoit shot out till it was twice its length, like a piece of pulled elastic. He hissed and puffed and then he threw . . . and missed.

'I WON!' cried Debbie.

The devil jumped around and fizzed till he looked like a firework. 'All right!' he spat. 'One all. Last round. And this time it's brain work. No more of this silly sport stuff.'

'Right!' said Debbie.

'Maths,' said the devil. 'We'll go up to your room where nobody'll disturb us and have a maths competition to settle it.'

'How old did you say you were?' said Debbie.

'Five thousand.'

'And I'm eight and a half. So you've had . . . um . . . four thousand nine hundred and ninety-one and a half years more than I have to learn maths in.'

'Scared?' jeered the devil.

'No. I am not!' shouted Debbie.

They went up to her room and Debbie shut the door firmly. Downstairs, her mother called up, 'What are you up to Debbie?' and Debbie called back, 'Nothing, Mum. Just doing some homework.'

Debbie and the devil sat down at either side of the table. Debbie waited until the devil was looking the other way and then slipped her school calculator out of her jeans pocket and held it on her knee where he couldn't see it.

'We take it in turns to set the questions,' said the devil. 'First to answer wins the round. First to win two in a row is the outright winner. This is it! I start. Seven times eight!'

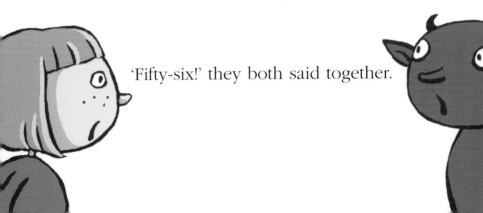

'Fifty-six!' they both said together.

'Eighteen plus six!' cried Debbie.

'Twenty-four!' snapped the devil, just ahead. 'One to me! Gotcha! My go. Two times three times four!'

'Twenty-four again!' shouted Debbie, almost before he had finished.

The devil blew out a great spout of flame. 'Right! Now let's see who's so clever . . . Last question. Quick!'

'Three hundred and forty-eight times five hundred and ninety-seven,' said Debbie loudly and slowly and clearly.

The devil's eyes gleamed. He spat some more flame. '*Now* who's being a bit too clever,' he said. '*Now* who's going to get what's coming to them! Um . . . three sevens are twenty-one, carry two, three nines are . . . '

Debbie's fingers tapped away. She glanced down. 'Two hundred and seven thousand seven hundred and fifty-six!'

The devil glared. He went on muttering and counting on his fingers. And then he gave a great howl of fury. He howled and jumped and gnashed his teeth. His tail whirled around, the whole room was filled with flying sparks. He spat flame so that Debbie had to duck down under the table. And then he started to get smaller. And as he shrank he howled . . .

a howl that trailed away as the devil himself began to disappear. He got smaller and smaller until there was nothing on the other side of the table but a little red thing like a coal still spitting and smoking. And then with a final bleep and a flash he was gone.

Where he has gone is a secret. Whether or not he will come back nobody knows. As for Debbie, she was now one of the very few people to have tricked a devil, so she went down and ate a very large tea to celebrate.

THE
MONSTER FROM
UNDERGROUND

GILLIAN CROSS
Illustrated by Chris Priestley

To Anthony
G.C.

For Glenn
C.P.

Chapter One

BOMBER WILSON WAS brilliant. He was a
wonderful footballer, a star at snooker and a
genius at video games. He knew about
computers and aeroplanes and dinosaurs and
he had the best bicycle in the whole school.

But he HATED writing.

Whenever Mrs Evans, his teacher, said, 'Get out your pens,' Bomber shuddered. He could never write more than a quarter of a page, about anything. After that, his hand ached from holding the pen, and his brain ached even more.

So he was horrified when Mrs Evans told them about the Nature Diary.

'First,' she said, 'choose something to watch for a week. Write a little bit about it every day – just before you go to bed.'

For a week! Bomber shuddered.

'Can we watch anything we like?' said Kevin.

Harriet Newton tossed her head. '*I'm* going to make a rain gauge to put in my garden. Then I can write about the weather every day. How much rain there's been and –'

'I'll watch my dog,' Paul
said, interrupting. They
all interrupted Harriet,
because she never stopped.
'I'll notice what he does
every day.'

Mrs Evans beamed. 'That's
the idea. Watch for seven days –
and keep an open mind. Then at
the end of the week, write down
what you've learnt. There'll be
a prize for the best one.'

Seven days' writing! At home! Bomber sat and glowered as everyone chattered about the Diaries. And by the end of the day, he was the only person in the class who hadn't had an idea.

'Look for something interesting on your way home,' Mrs Evans said.

So he looked hard. And what he saw was the road works.

They were making a cutting through Hawthorn Hill, for the new motorway, and all the different

levels of rock showed. Just like layers in a slice of cake, except that each layer of rock was older than the one above.

Bomber stared at them. Those rocks had been hidden under the ground for millions and millions of years and suddenly there they were, up on top again. Now that *was* interesting.

And perhaps he could write about it in his Nature Diary! He grinned and got the book out, to make a sketch.

But Harriet was right behind him, and she hooted with laughter. 'Hey, everyone! Bomber's going to write a Nature Diary about a *road works*!'

'It's the rocks not the road works,' said Bomber.

But Harriet didn't listen. She just laughed louder. 'Watch those diggers, Bomber! Perhaps one of them will have a dear little baby digger! Or spin a web and catch an aeroplane!'

'Shut up!' said Bomber.

But Harriet went on about vegetarian tractors and wild, meat-eating diggers, all the way home. And it *was* all the way, because she lived next door to Bomber.

So he didn't have a moment to think about his Nature Diary.

Chapter Two

THE NEXT DAY was Tuesday, and Mrs Evans
kept nagging him about choosing something
for the Diary. But he couldn't think of a thing.

To make it worse, Harriet spent all day
teasing him about diggers. She even kept it up
while they walked home, which made him rush
past the road works without stopping.

And that was a pity, because the machines
had opened up a whole new layer since the day
before. Quite a different sort of rock, with some
strange, interesting-looking lumps in it. But
Bomber didn't look properly, because of Harriet.

When he got home – there was Harriet's mother, drinking coffee and going on about the rain gauge.

Bomber's mother frowned as he came in. 'What are *you* doing for this Nature Diary, Bernard?'

'I'm still deciding.' Bomber shuffled his feet.

Mrs Newton rattled on without taking any notice, just like Harriet.

' . . . and she checks that gauge every five minutes, to see how much rain she's collected. I had to *make* her go to bed last night.'

That was when Bomber had his idea. If Mrs Newton *made* Harriet go to bed at night – he would do his Nature Diary then! He could slip out every night, at midnight, and do a survey of the night sky! If he did it at night, he wouldn't have to put up with Harriet laughing at him over the fence.

Brilliant! He didn't tell his mother, of course, but he set the alarm on his watch straight away.

It woke him up at a quarter to midnight, beeping quietly in his ear. By five to twelve he was standing in the back garden, looking up at the sky.

Half the sky. The other half was hidden by the Newtons' apple tree. He needed to climb higher to get a proper view. Standing on the rubbish heap, he scrambled on to the shed roof and took a good look around.

That was when he saw them.

There were three roundish grey things, lying in a patch of moonlight in the middle of Harriet's lawn. They were as big as footballs, but not quite ball-shaped. More like eggs.

Eggs? How could they be? What creature laid eggs the size of footballs?

All the lights were off in the Newtons' house. Quietly, Bomber slid down into their garden and walked across the lawn, to have a better look at the strange grey objects.

They were definitely eggs. Huge, *enormous* eggs. He put out his hand to feel the shells, but just before he touched them he noticed something else. Something that made him snatch his hand back, as fast as he could.

Footprints.

There were two of them. They were at least half a metre long, and deep as well, as if they'd been made by something very heavy.

Between them was a long, deep groove, like the mark of a dragging tail.

Except that this tail had to be the size of a tree trunk.

Bomber stared. It was frightening, standing next to those giant eggs and looking at those enormous footprints – but it was a brilliant chance to begin his Nature Diary. He began to sketch the eggs and the footprints, as fast as he could.

Then a voice hissed behind him. 'What are you doing?'

He turned round and saw Harriet, glaring at him.

'Have you been fiddling with my rain gauge?' she snapped.

'Your rain gauge?' Bomber almost laughed. 'Who cares about that? Just look at these amazing eggs. And the footprints.'

'Eggs?' Harriet said. 'Footprints? What are you talking about?'

'You must be blind! Can't you see –' Bomber whirled around, to point at them – and stopped dead.

There was only the empty lawn. The eggs and the footprints had vanished.

Chapter Three

THE NEXT DAY, Harriet's father came round as soon as he got home from work. To complain.

'Bernard's been tampering with Harriet's rain gauge.'

It was no use arguing. Bomber's mother wouldn't listen. She lost her temper and sent him straight to bed.

Bomber pulled a face, but he was really quite tired. He lay down on the bed to read a comic and fell asleep at once, without undressing or pulling the curtains.

When his alarm went off at a quarter to twelve, he woke up and blinked. For a moment he couldn't think what was going on, because he had forgotten all about the survey of the night sky. And then, suddenly, he was wide awake.

Something had moved, just outside the window.

There was no shape to be seen. Just darkness. But the darkness had rippled and *moved*.

For a few seconds, Bomber was too frightened to breathe. Then the rippling happened again.

Very slowly, as if something was crawling past
the window. On and on and on.

But it was an *upstairs* window! What was
huge enough to block that? It would have to
be bigger than an elephant!

Whatever it was, it wasn't looking in. Quietly
he crawled out of bed and crept over to the
window. Pressing his nose to the glass, he
peered out at the stuff that was passing. It was
rough and wrinkled, a bit like an elephant's

skin. And where the moonlight caught it, he could see blotches and streaks.

Bomber's heart thudded with fright, but he wouldn't let himself run back to bed. Whatever the creature was, it was much too big to get into the room. It was worth trying to get a better look at it.

Carefully, Bomber pulled down the window catch. It squeaked a bit, but whatever was outside didn't take any notice. The skin just went on rippling past as he pushed the window open.

The smell nearly
knocked him over.

It was like old grass
cuttings and rotting
plants, mixed with
mushrooms and stale
cabbage.

Bomber clapped
his hand over his nose
but, before he could recover, the door behind
him was flung open. His mother appeared in

her dressing gown,
looking angry.

'Bernard, what
are you doing? You
woke me up from
a deep sleep!'

Hadn't she
noticed the smell?
Bomber waved at
the window. 'Look!'

'At what?' said
his mother.

Bomber turned back to the window, but there was no smell any more. No rough, blotchy skin. Just the dark sky, with the moon shining through the Newtons' apple tree.

The giant whatever-it-was had vanished.

His mother made him go to bed at once, but the moment she was out of the way, he switched on his bedside light. Very strange things were happening, and he wanted to make sure he remembered them. Grabbing his Nature Diary, he started to write.

I have just seen something very peculiar outside my window . . .

Chapter Four

ON THURSDAY, BOMBER made a plan. He knew it was no use trying to tell people about the eggs and the wrinkled skin and the giant footprints. No one would believe a word of it.

He needed a witness.

Next time something strange happened, there had to be someone else there. Not one of his friends. Someone who wouldn't back him up unless he was telling the truth.

And he knew the ideal person.

At twenty to twelve that night, he was standing in the Newtons' back garden, throwing little stones up at Harriet's window to wake her up.

It worked brilliantly, because the window was open. Harriet stuck her head out, looking furious.

'*Bomber?* What's going on? That hit me on the nose.'

'Sssh!' Bomber said. 'Come down.'

'Why? If you've touched my rain gauge –'

Bomber didn't bother to answer. He just backed away from the window and waited, staring up at the big, bright moon behind the apple tree. After a few minutes, Harriet crept through the back door.

'Are you crazy?' she hissed. 'My dad'll go berserk if he catches you in our garden again. What do you want?'

'Wait a bit, and I'll show you,' muttered Bomber. 'And be quiet.'

They waited. They stood with their backs to the house, staring down the hill. Far below, they could see the motorway road works but even those were still and quiet.

'It's funny,' Harriet whispered. 'Everything's very bright, but there's no moon.'

'Yes there is,' said Bomber. 'Up behind the apple tree. It –'

And then he stopped. Because she was right. There wasn't a moon behind the apple tree, and there weren't any stars either. Instead, there was a big, black patch, as if something was standing between them and the sky. Something huge.

'Harriet –'

But before he could warn her, the black shape moved and they saw it properly. The monster. It had a vast, humped body and a long, thick neck that reared up into the sky. Its head looked ridiculously small as it peered over the top of the house.

Harriet gasped. She clutched at Bomber's arm and he clutched hers.

Slowly, the small head swayed from side to side, and they caught a whiff of the mushroomy, rotten-grass smell.

Then Harriet gulped. 'Look at the apple tree!'

The creature's head bent down to grab at the top of the tree and the leaves shook, furiously.

When the head reared up again, there were black, leafy shapes sticking out of its mouth. A slow crunching, chomping sound came from somewhere up in the sky.

Bomber didn't dare to move, but he stared at the little head and the long, long neck. They reminded him of something. If only he could work out what . . .

And then – it vanished.

Suddenly, there was nothing there, except the big, white moon, behind the black branches of the apple tree. Harriet took a deep breath.

'What *was* it?'

'I don't know,' said Bomber. 'But I'm certainly going to find out.'

When he got back to his bedroom, he wrote down all the details, underneath what he had written the day before.

. . . its body must have been six or seven metres high, and its neck reached even higher. It was a very long, thin neck, with a small head . . .

He lay awake for hours, trying to think where he had seen a neck and a head like that. But his brain refused to work. He fell asleep at half past four, without having remembered.

But when he woke up the next morning, he *knew*.

He jumped out of bed and rummaged in the bottom of his wardrobe. There was a great

heap of polythene bags in there, full of old toys
and games. Building bricks. Plastic aeroplanes.
Model soldiers with their trucks and weapons.
And somewhere . . .

The bag he was looking for was right at the
bottom. He tugged it out and emptied it on to
the floor.

There were dozens of little plastic dinosaurs,
all different shapes and colours. He shuffled
through them, tossing away the stegosaurus and
the tyrannosaurus, the parasaurolophus and the
iguanadon.

And suddenly, there was the one he was looking for. He gazed at the long neck and the little head for a moment, and then turned it over to read the name underneath, to make sure he was right.

DIPLODOCUS.

Standing it on his bedside table, he sketched the shape carefully in his Nature Diary. Then he pushed it into his pocket. All the way to school, his fingers were curled round the thick body, feeling the long, long neck and the long, long tail.

Was it *possible*?

As he passed the road works, he stopped for a minute or two, to look at the layers of rock in the cutting. The bottom layer was a long way down. It must be very old. And he could still see those strange lumps in it . . .

When he got to school, he didn't say anything to Harriet. He just took out the diplodocus and pushed it into her hand.

She stared. 'But that's impossible. They've been extinct for millions of years.'

'I know,' Bomber said. 'But look at it.'

Harriet looked down at the dinosaur again. 'Nobody will believe us,' she said. 'Unless we can prove it. How about a photograph?'

Bomber stared. Then, for the first time ever, he smiled at her. 'Brilliant! Let's do it tonight.'

Chapter Five

THEY MET IN Harriet's back garden just before midnight, both carrying their cameras.

'We'll get better pictures if we're high up,' muttered Harriet. 'Because the creature's so big. Let's climb onto your shed.'

They knelt on the roof, side by side, with the cameras held ready. At first they thought nothing was going to happen, but after ten minutes, Bomber nudged Harriet.

The apple tree was shaking. The fluttering leaves showed up clearly, with the full moon

behind them. And then, slowly – very slowly –
the huge black shape of the diplodocus began
to move.

Bomber shivered. Suppose the monster saw
them? Suppose it knocked the shed over?
Suppose –

But it was no good thinking about that. If
they wanted photographs, they had to stay there.
He forced himself to hold the camera steady.

'Now!' hissed Harriet.

Both cameras flashed at once. The light was
like an explosion, much brighter than Bomber
had expected. It must have surprised the
diplodocus too. Slowly, but not quite as slowly
as before, it moved again – towards them.

Its head reared up, on top of its long neck,
and began to sway from side to side, searching.
Getting closer and closer. Harriet gulped.

'Let's get out of here!'

Bomber shook his head. 'Wait. I don't think
it'll hurt us. It's supposed to be a vegetarian.'
Crossing his fingers hard, he hoped all those
scientists were right.

The head swayed closer and closer. It was small for such a huge animal – but it looked enormous as it came down towards them. Lower and lower it bent, until Bomber and Harriet were looking straight into its eyes.

The eyes of a dinosaur.

They were very pale, like pools of rainwater, and empty. Bomber stared deep into them. He couldn't tell whether the diplodocus saw them, but he was too scared to move.

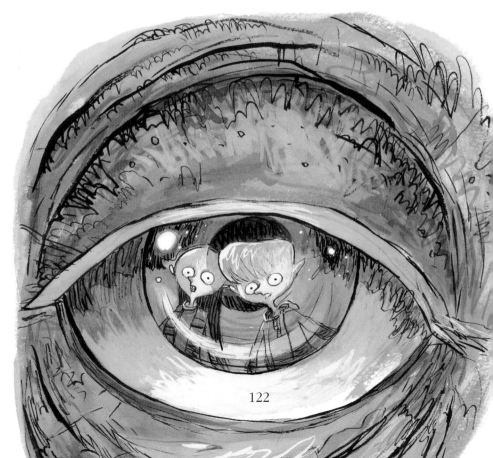

Then Harriet grabbed his arm. 'Photos!' she whispered. 'We'll never get another chance like this.'

Both together, they lifted their cameras. Bomber got the focus right and made sure the dinosaur's head was in the centre of his viewfinder. Then he said, 'Now!'

And the flashes went off together.

What happened then was mind-boggling.

Bomber wrote it all down in his Nature Diary the next morning.

. . . when the lights flashed, the dinosaur began to move towards us again. We couldn't escape, because it was too close. For one second, we could see it lurching forwards and then everything went dark and very strange. Tingling.

The diplodocus walked straight through us.

Chapter Six

HARRIET GOT THE photos developed on Saturday morning, and she took them straight round to Bomber's. When he opened the door, he could see that she was upset.

'What's the matter, Harry?'

'It's these. Look.' She held out the photographs.

There were four beautiful pictures of the full moon behind the apple tree – but no sign of a dinosaur in any of them.

'There's nothing there,' said Harriet. 'Did we imagine it?'

Bomber shook his head. 'I don't think so. Come down to the road works. I want to show you something.'

They walked down together to the cutting in Hawthorn Hill and stared at the layers of rock. Like layers in a slice of cake – except that each one was older than the one above.

'The bottom layer must be very old indeed,' Harriet said slowly.

Bomber nodded. 'About a hundred and fifty million years.'

'And those strange, enormous lumps?'

'Bones,' said Bomber. 'I reckon.'

Harriet frowned. 'Someone ought to have a look at them.'

'I've been thinking about that,' said Bomber. 'I think I'll write to the local paper.'

'Write? *You?*'

Harriet hooted with laughter, but Bomber just grinned.

Chapter Seven

TWO WEEKS LATER, Bomber finished his
Nature Diary. First he pasted in the best of his
newspaper cuttings. There was a large
photograph of his face and underneath it said:

Bernard 'Bomber' Wilson

Diplodocus

SCHOOLBOY'S DINOSAUR FIND

Schoolboy Bernard Wilson (above left) has
sharp eyes! He noticed some strange lumps
in the excavation for the new M39 and wrote
to his local paper about them. Now scientists
believe that the lumps are fossilized bones of a
diplodocus (above right) – a huge dinosaur that
has been extinct for millions of years.

There was a sketch of the diplodocus, too. The artist had got the face a bit wrong and drawn the skin all scaly, but it was definitely the creature they had seen in Harriet's garden.

When he had stuck the cutting in, Bomber read through the whole Diary again. He was amazed to see how much he had written. There was only one page left, and he knew what had to go on that. Picking up his pen, he began to write.

WHAT I'VE LEARNT

I'm sure we saw a diplodocus. Not a real one, because someone else would have noticed that. And a live diplodocus couldn't have walked through us.

I think it was a ghost. It started walking when its bones came to the surface in the road works. And it's stopped now the bones have been discovered.

I've thought a lot about this, Mrs Evans. Keeping an open mind, like you said. And I can't see any other explanation.

Mrs Evans was delighted with Bomber's Diary.

Well done! she wrote underneath. *It's crazy but it's brilliant. And at last you've managed to write a lot!*

And she gave him two gold stars and a special prize for the Most Original Entry.

She didn't say she believed Bomber's story,
but she kept the newspaper cutting and
promised the class a trip to see the dinosaur.

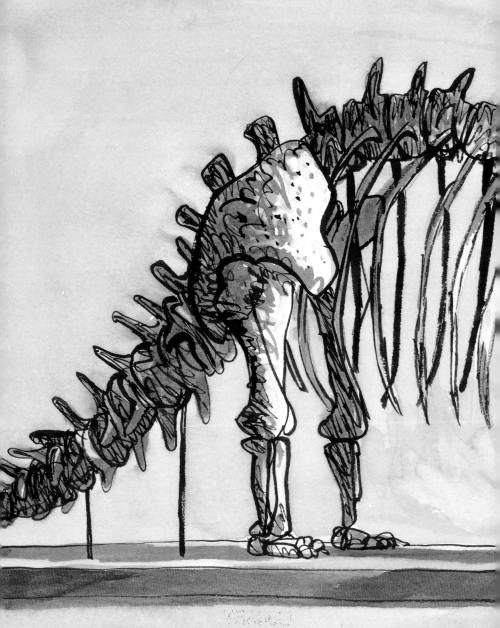

Diplodocus

If you enjoyed reading these stories,
try these tasty tales!

MICHAEL MORPURGO

Animal Tales

Three stories in one

EGMONT PRESS: ETHICAL PUBLISHING

Egmont Press is about turning writers into successful authors and children into passionate readers – producing books that enrich and entertain. As a responsible children's publisher, we go even further, considering the world in which our consumers are growing up.

Safety First
Naturally, all of our books meet legal safety requirements. But we go further than this; every book with play value is tested to the highest standards – if it fails, it's back to the drawing-board.

Made Fairly
We are working to ensure that the workers involved in our supply chain – the people that make our books – are treated with fairness and respect.

Responsible Forestry
We are committed to ensuring all our papers come from environmentally and socially responsible forest sources.

For more information, please visit our website at
www.egmont.co.uk/ethicalpublishing